THE FAMILY TREE

WRITTEN BY SEAN DIXON

& ILLUSTRATED BY LILY SNOWDEN-FINE

FROM AN IDEA BY KATERINA CIZEK

tundra

The handout was a drawing of a tree. A strong, beautiful oak. Ada's teacher had drawn it herself.

Ada looked a little closer, and her face fell.

That evening, Ada did not want to go to bed.

The next morning, Ada did not want to get up.

Her parents were worried. "Is there anything bothering you at school, bunny?"

Ada showed them the tree. They looked a little closer. Their faces fell.

"It's due on Monday," said Ada.

"Why don't we go upstairs and talk to Rosie about it?" said her mom.

"I think she had a similar problem."

Thursday evening, Ada went upstairs with her mom and dad to see their friend Kim and her daughter, Rosie.

"I got one of those last year," said Rosie. "But it's just my mom and me. I was a What-If baby."

"She means IVF," said Kim.

"What-If you're by yourself and you really want a baby?
Then the birds and the bees have to get doctor's degrees."
"So what did you do instead of a tree?" said Ada.
"We drew a wild rose," Rosie said. "Here, I can show you."

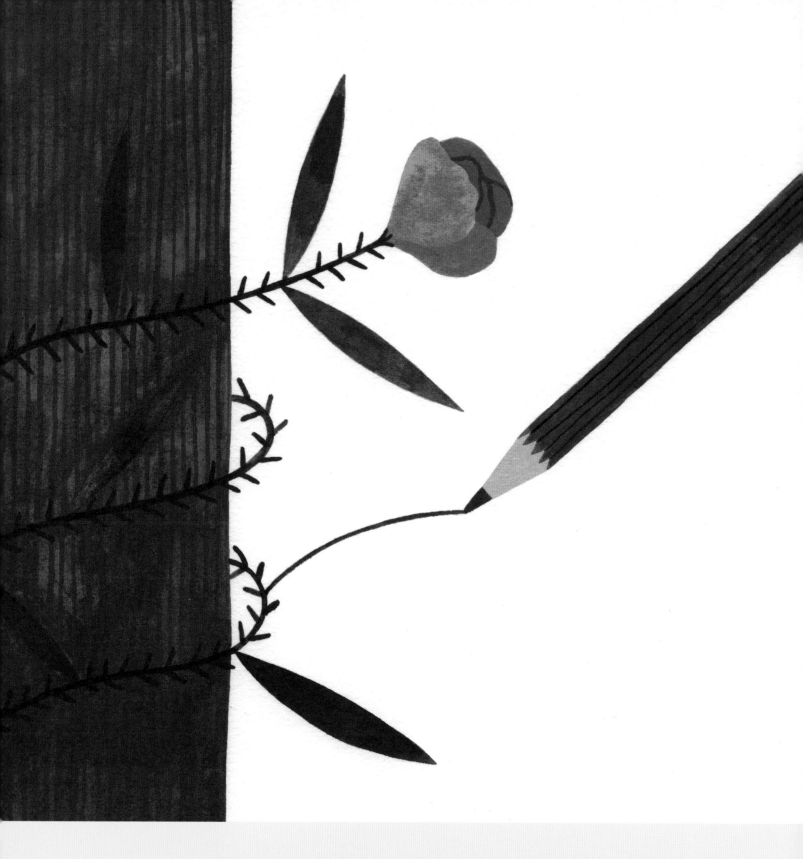

"It's pretty," said Ada.

"See that flower? That's me!" Rosie said. "My mom is the strong climbing vine, and everyone else that helped — like a father or something — they're part of the root system. It's underground, so I can't see it, but I know it's there."

"Rosie wrapped a flower around my tree," Ada said later.

"You like that?" asked her mom.

"It makes me feel a little bit better," Ada replied.

"A little bit?" said her dad. "Well, why don't we go talk to Bessie and Tess tomorrow?"

On Friday afternoon, they visited Ada's former foster parents, Bessie and Tess. Tess was Bessie's mother.

Ada laid out her tree with the flower on it.

Two boys wandered out of a bedroom.

"Bessie said you used to live here," one of them said.

"Yeah, I did," said Ada.

"So I guess you're our foster sister," he said.

"I guess I am," she replied.

"I'm Miles."

"Ada."

"I'm Alex."

"What's that?" asked Miles.

"It's supposed to be my family tree," Ada said.

"Can we be in it?" said Miles.

"Sure."

"What are you drawing?" Ada asked.

"I'm drawing islands," said Miles. "That's yours with your tree. This is mine."

"Can I draw an island too?" Alex asked.

"My island has nests for all the birds that are going to want to come and be a family with me," said Miles.

Alex picked up a green crayon. "My island is a turtle and that turtle is me . . .

. . . so I have a home no matter what."

"But we're still all connected," Miles said.

"Yeah, we're an atoll," Ada replied.

"What's an atoll?" asked Alex.

"It's an island chain made out of coral," said Ada. "We learned about them in school. They look separated but they're not."

"Did you like those kids?
Were they nice?"
"Yeah," said Ada.
"They were nice."

Saturday morning, Ada and her parents went to see Uncle Michael and
Uncle Ben and their five-year-old, Leo.

"Interesting," said Uncle Michael. "Islands."

"It started out as just a tree," said Ada.

"I like the river idea better," said Leo.

"The river idea?"

"It's where Da and Pa and Ellen and Auntie Mika are all rivers that empty into the ocean of ME."

"Who is Ellen? And who is Auntie Mika?" asked Ada.

"Ellen carried me," said Leo. "She was my Sure-Is-Great."

"Surrogate, buddy," said Uncle Michael.

"And Auntie Mika is my sister," said Uncle Ben. "She donated the egg for Leo."

"Can you draw the rivers?" asked Ada.

"If you help," said Leo.

"And do you mind having islands in your ocean?"

"I don't mind if you don't mind," said Leo. "Let's make a forest for the rivers too!"

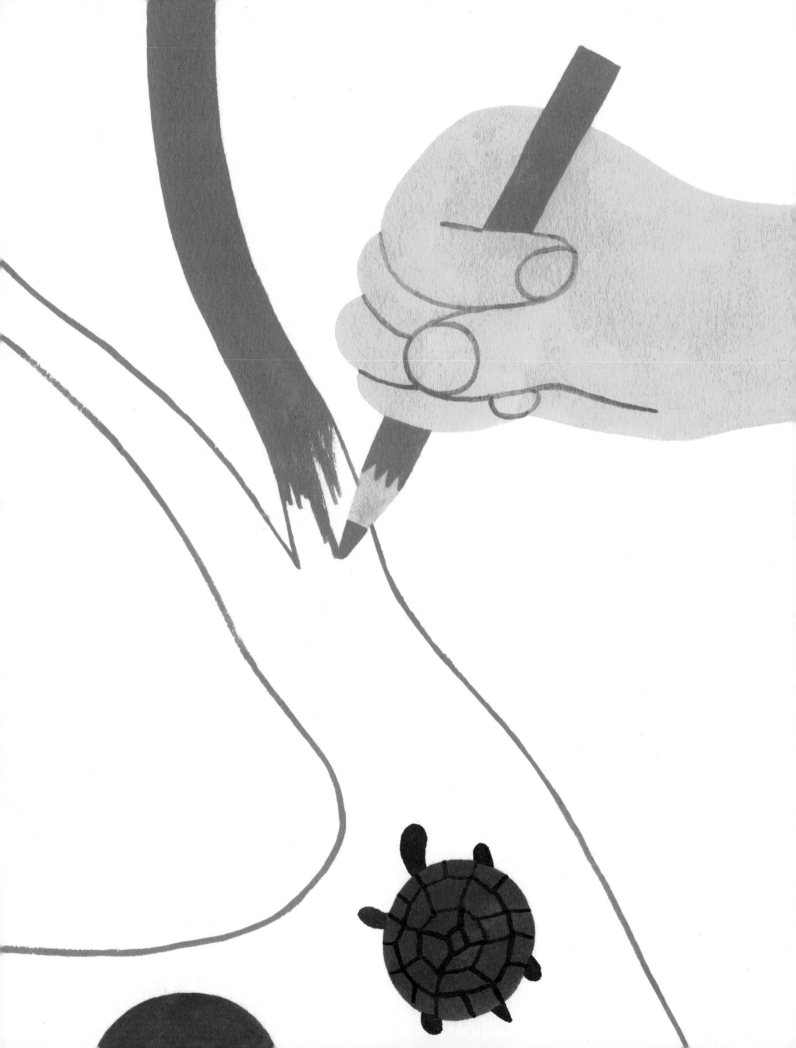

Saturday afternoon, Ada had a playdate with her friend Maev.
"Can I draw on it too?" Maev asked.

"What do you want to draw?" Ada said.

"I kind of want to make mole tunnels. See? I can put them here."

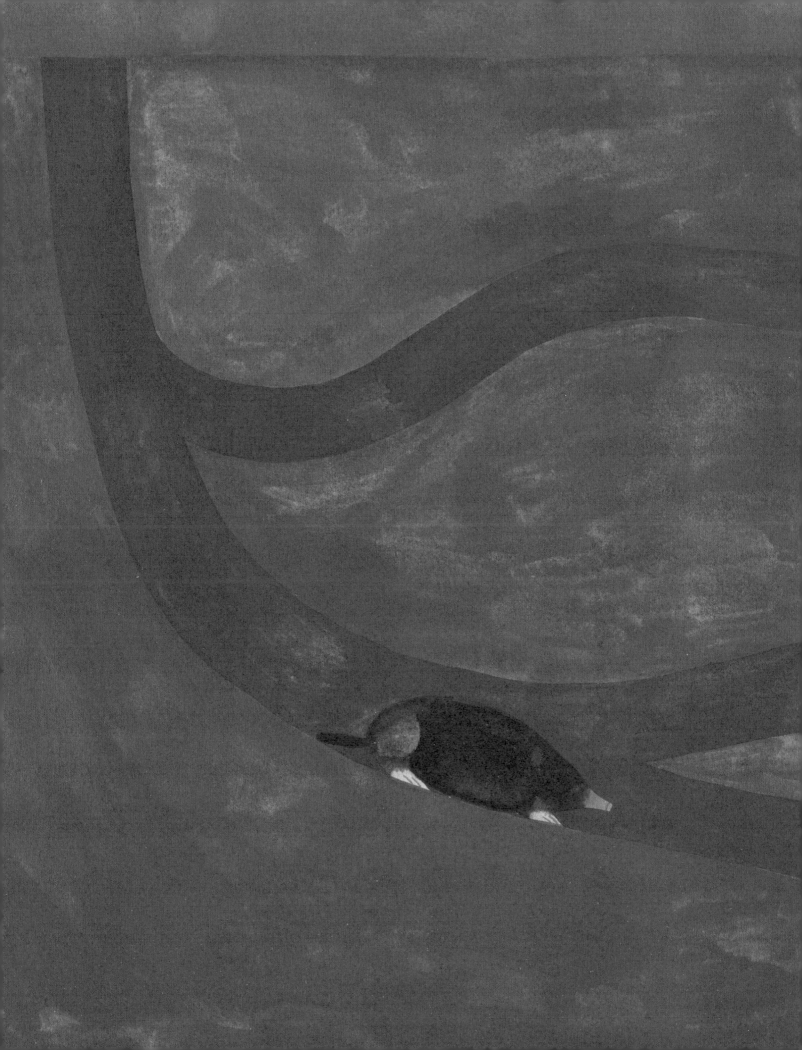

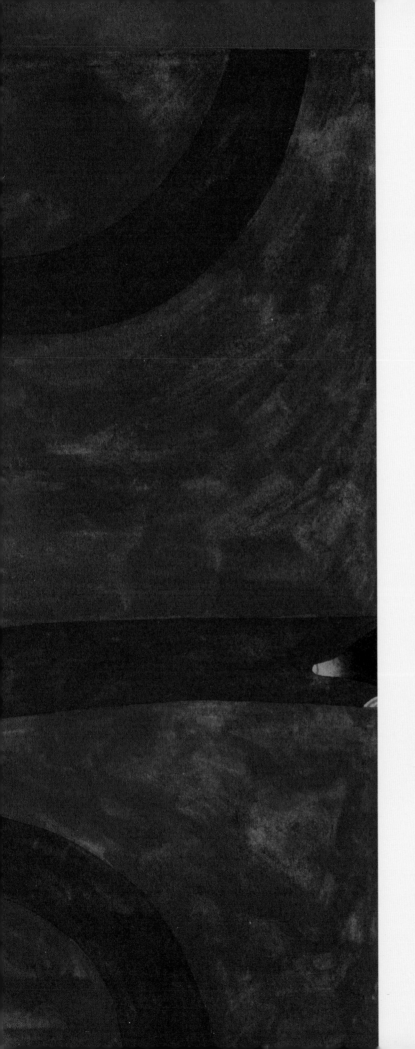

"Why mole tunnels?" asked Ada.
  "Sometimes I'm at my dad's
house; sometimes I'm here at my
mom's. I love being with my dad,
but when I'm there I sometimes
miss my sister, who just lives here.
So I wish I could sneak back
through a mole tunnel to just
say hello."

Ada studied her tree.
"There's still so much missing," she said.

"Don't forget we're going to see your sister tomorrow, bunny."
"Oh, yay! Yay!"

On Sunday, they went to visit Ada's little sister, Mia, who was only three.

Mia wasn't much interested in the family tree project, though she was interested in Ada.

"That's a nice tree," said Mia's mamá, Claudia.

"But I can see why you wanted more than the tree," said Mia's mutti, Gerta.

"Mia's got to be in there, because she's my sister. And you two have to be in there, because you're Mia's parents," said Ada. "But there's nowhere to put you in the tree."

"Mia, no, that's your sister's project!"

"No, that's okay," said Ada. "It looks like a big coastline."

"A coastline is a nice idea. Maybe Mia's abuelo and abuela could be down here," said Claudia. "Some wildflowers by the seashore?"

"And Mia's opa is way, far away in the opposite direction," said Gerta. "Wildflowers in the mountains."

"And we can be flowers somewhere in the middle," said Claudia, "sending our pollen back and forth, from the shore to the mountains, from the mountains to the shore."

"Pollen on a butterfly's wings!" said Ada.

"A monarch butterfly's wings!" said Gerta.

"I love it! Thank you, Claudia. Thank you, Gerta. Thank you, beautiful baby sister!"

When Ada got home, she had an oak tree with a rose, some wildflowers and a butterfly; a forest with mole tunnels underneath it; and a mountain range with two rivers flowing down from it into an ocean with an atoll and a southern shore with more wild flowers.

She wrote down all the names. She decided to add her teacher's name to the tree, since her teacher had drawn the tree. And she added some other islands for the foster brothers and sisters who had lived with her in the days before her adoption. She couldn't remember their names so she made them up.

"I only have one problem," Ada said. "I still don't know where to put us."

"You know," said Ada's dad, "some people make constellations of their families. Why don't we put us up there in the sky? That way you'll have a stellar view."

After Ada's work was done, it was dark.

The little family went and sat on the roof.

It was a full moon. Ada thought about all the people who made her feel like family.

"What's the matter, bunny?"

"I keep thinking about where to put Sochi."

"I was wondering when you were going to add Sochi."

"Why didn't Sochi keep me? What did I do?"
"You didn't do anything, bunny. Your birth mother
loves you and wants you to be taken care of."
"I must have done something."

"Do you think your sister, Mia, did something to
make Sochi not want to keep her?"
"No, because Mia was just a little baby, a beautiful
little baby! She could never have done anything!"
"You were just a beautiful baby too, bunny."

Ada was quiet for a while.

"I just wish I knew how to include her."

"Why don't you make Sochi the moon? The moon is always there, even if you don't always see it."

"That's true."
Ada looked at the moon and smiled.

Monday morning, Ada brought her finished family tree to school.

But it wasn't a tree . . .

To my daughter —SD

To my wonderful parents and my new family:
Adam and our cat, Charlie —LSF

Tundra Books, an imprint of Penguin Random House Canada Young Readers,
a division of Penguin Random House of Canada Limited

Library and Archives Canada Cataloguing in Publication

Title: The family tree / Sean Dixon ; [illustrations by] Lily Snowden-Fine.
Names: Dixon, Sean (Playwright), author. | Snowden-Fine, Lily, illustrator.
Identifiers: Canadiana (print) 20200409700 | Canadiana (ebook) 20200410997
  ISBN 9780735267664 (hardcover) | ISBN 9780735267671 (EPUB)
Classification: LCC PS8557.I97 F36 2022 | DDC jC813/.54—dc23

Published simultaneously in the United States of America by Tundra Books of Northern
New York, an imprint of Penguin Random House Canada Young Readers, a division of
Penguin Random House of Canada Limited

Library of Congress Control Number: 2020951505

Edited by Samantha Swenson
Designed by John Martz
The artwork in this book was painted with gouache and edited to remove all of Charlie's fur.
The text was set in Bembo.

Printed in China

www.penguinrandomhouse.ca

1   2   3   4   5   26   25   24   23   22

Penguin
Random House
TUNDRA BOOKS